Sometimes It's
Grandmas and Grandpas
Not Mommies and Daddies

To Jazzy,
My wonderfully special
and blessedly normal granddaughter.
I love you.
GB
(Nonnie)

To Betty.
Devoted Grandma.
Cherished Mom.
With love,
MLH

Editor: Cynthia Vance   Production Editor: Briana Green
Production Manager: Louise Kurtz   Designer: Freeform Studio

First edition
10 9 8 7 6 5 4 3 2

Library of Congress Cataloging-in-Publication Data

Byrne, Gayle.
   Sometimes it's grandmas and grandpas, not mommies and daddies / text by Gayle Byrne; illustrations by Mary Haverfield. — 1st ed.
       p. cm.
   Summary: A young girl who lives with her grandparents experiences warmth, love, and closeness, even when she wonders why her parents are not raising her.
   ISBN 978-0-7892-1028-9 (hardcover : alk. paper) [1. Grandparents—Fiction.]
I. Haverfield, Mary, ill. II. Title. III. Title: Sometimes it is grandmas and grandpas, not mommies and daddies.

PZ7.B993So 2009
[E]—dc22

                                            2009005854

For bulk and premium sales and for text adoption procedures, write to Customer Service Manager, Abbeville Press, 137 Varick Street, New York, NY 10013, or call 1-800-ARTBOOK.

Visit Abbeville Kids online at www.abbevillefamily.com.

Sometimes It's
Grandmas and Grandpas
Not Mommies and Daddies

Text by
Gayle Byrne

Illustrations by
Mary Haverfield

Abbeville Kids
An Imprint of Abbeville Press
New York & London

We cuddle a lot together,
Nonnie and me.

S ometimes
it's 'cuz morning comes too soon
and I'm still sleepy
and Nonnie snuggles in bed with me
'cuz she's sleepy too.

S ometimes it's 'cuz I'm going to my school,
and I'll be with Miss Heidi and Miss Robyn
and Maddie and Morgan and Charlie and
the two Zacharys

Miss Heidi

Miss Robyn

Maddie

Charlie

Morgan

The two Zacharys

and the day s-t-r-e-t-c-h-e-s like forever and ever

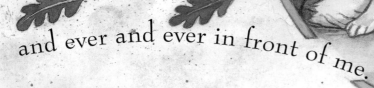

and ever and ever in front of me.

W e cuddle a lot together,
Nonnie and me.
Sometimes it's 'cuz it's been a long time
since breakfast and I've been at school
and Nonnie's been at work
and it feels so good to be
together again.

S ometimes it's 'cuz it's
    cold and wintery outside
and our house is warm and has
    cooking-supper smells.

Sometimes Poppy is with us and
we're all on the couch watching
George and the man with the yellow hat.
And Poppy says I'm a curious monkey, too.

Sometimes Buddy is with us
and we're on the big bed—
Nonnie and Poppy's bed—
talking puppy-talk and rubbing puppy ears,
telling stories and reading stories
turning pages
and Nonnie says, "I wonder
what happens next."

Sometimes it's 'cuz there's a Daddy
in the story we're reading and
he's twirling and spinning his baby girl and
their mouths are wide open laughing.
And I wonder if my Daddy and I will ever do that.

And on the next page there's a Mommy
and it's nighttime and there are stars
up in the sky and a skinny piece of moon.
And the Mommy is tucking her big girl in her
big-girl bed, all pink and purple, and I wonder
why my Mommy doesn't do that.

We cuddle a lot together,
Nonnie and me.
'Cuz sometimes it's Nonnies and Poppys
that take care of
baby girls and big girls and
baby boys and big boys,
not Mommies and Daddies.

I climb on
Nonnie's lap
and put my small hand
in her big hand
and rub the bumps on top.
And I put my nose in her neck and
smell her Nonnie smell
and Nonnie holds me tight and
tells me in a whisper,
"We're two lucky girls."
'Cuz Poppies can twirl and spin
just as good as Daddies.

And Nonnies tuck little kids
in their little beds
and big kids in their big beds
just as good as Mommies.

And 'cuz
hugs and cuddles never run out
at home with Nonnie and Poppy.

AUTHOR'S NOTE

I remember so clearly the day my granddaughter and I were reading a picture book, and for the first time I realized how puzzling our life together might seem to her. It was a story about a Mommy and her little baby bunny looking out the window, waiting for the Daddy bunny to come home. My granddaughter sat for a moment, processing the scene in her young two-year-old mind, trying to relate it to her own world. She tilted her head, looking up at me, her nose crinkled. A look of innocent confusion crossed her face.

I knew the child cuddling in my lap had a valid and valuable story too. And that story was nowhere to be found in any of the books in the library or bookstore. It was a story that needed to be written, and I knew from living in this different kind of family that I could write this different kind of story.

Sometimes It's Grandmas and Grandpas is this story. By demonstrating the unconditional love and support that can come from grandparents or other primary caregivers, it will help children understand their own family experience and teach them that not all happy families are alike!

—Gayle Byrne

Learn more about
GRANDFAMILIES:

Grandparents Raising Grandchildren
www.raisingyourgrandchildren.com

National Center on Grandparents Raising Grandchildren
http://chhs.gsu.edu/nationalcenter/

GrandFamilies of America
www.grandfamiliesofamerica.com

AARP Grandparent Information Center
www.aarp.org/families/grandparents/raising_grandchild/